A NOTE ABOUT THE STORY

Magic Spring came to Nami Rhee, as folktales traditionally have, in the form of a story told out loud. Handed down in her family from generation to generation, this is the story the author remembers most vividly from her childhood in Seoul. It is, she says, like ``a beautiful dream that I would like to keep forever.''

Here is a folktale rich in traditional Korean values: hard work is rewarded, greed and nastiness are punished. But unlike so many folk stories, in which the punishment is harsh and often violent, this tale extends the grace of a second chance to the villain as well as the hero. Everyone truly gets his or her just deserts.

Nami Rhee created the art for this book using handmade Korean rice paper and Korean ink and watercolor. Although she is an accomplished designer and draftsman, she says that when she began to execute the pictures her focus was on painting what she felt, rather than what she saw. The result is an expression of real emotion as well as painterly skill.

Readers will notice Korean characters positioned alongside the English text. These are phrases and excerpts from the story, that the author has translated so that children may see the beauty of Korean writing. If children listening to this tale are lucky enough, they will also have someone around who can pronounce such musical phrases as *yinnal yinnal eh*… (``*once upon a time*'').

—Tomie dePaola, Creative Director
WHITEBIRD BOOKS

**To my two best companions: Soovin, my sweetest daughter,
and Sungyong, my supportive husband**

I would also like to thank Arthur for finding me for this book,
and Gunta for helping me through.

Magic Spring

A KOREAN FOLKTALE
RETOLD AND ILLUSTRATED BY
NAMI RHEE

A WHITEBIRD BOOK
G. P. Putnam's Sons

옛날 옛날에 Once upon a time, at the edge of a village lived a kind old man and his wife. Though the man was so old that his beard was white as snow and his back was bent like an arch, he went every day to cut wood in the forest, for he had no child to help him. And every day the old woman sewed for hours, alone in the house, for she had no child by her side.

이웃의 욕심쟁이는 Their neighbor was a greedy old man who was so wealthy he could hire servants to do his bidding. When he saw the old man struggling with his axe, he would laugh and say, "Ha! Old Man, where is your son to help you?" He sneered at the old woman's patched-up clothes.

But the old couple never complained, not even to each other.

숲속에 파랑새 한마리가

One beautiful spring day the old man went to the middle of the forest to cut wood. The wind blew softly, and the sun tilted lazily between the branches of the trees. "It is too lovely to start work just yet," he thought, and sat for a moment on a nearby stump.

Just then a tiny bluebird landed on a branch not a yard from the old man. Her singing was so sweet and pure; each note was like a drop of rain. The old man quickly forgot everything else.

파랑새를 따라서 Then, suddenly, the bird flew away to another tree. The old man followed, moving quickly to the bird's new perch. But as soon as he caught up, the bird flew farther away and continued her song.

Once again the old man followed the bird: through the woods, over the stream, up one side of a mountain and down again. And the old man kept following, drawn by the silver lure of notes.

마침내 Finally, with a flash of blue wing against a broad expanse of green, the bird flew into a valley. Landing on a broad, flat rock, she cocked her head at the old man and continued to sing. With a few more steps, huffing and puffing, the old man caught up.

샘물을 마시고 나니

As he caught his breath, the old man noticed a small spring flowing between the rocks. He was so thirsty, no water had ever seemed more clear or inviting.

Cupping his hands, he brought a cold mouthful to his lips, and the sensation was like nothing he'd ever felt. It was as if the water had splashed, ice-clean, over every part of him at once.

He lay down on the grass, and even his long-bent back seemed to relax and uncurl as he fell into a deep sleep.

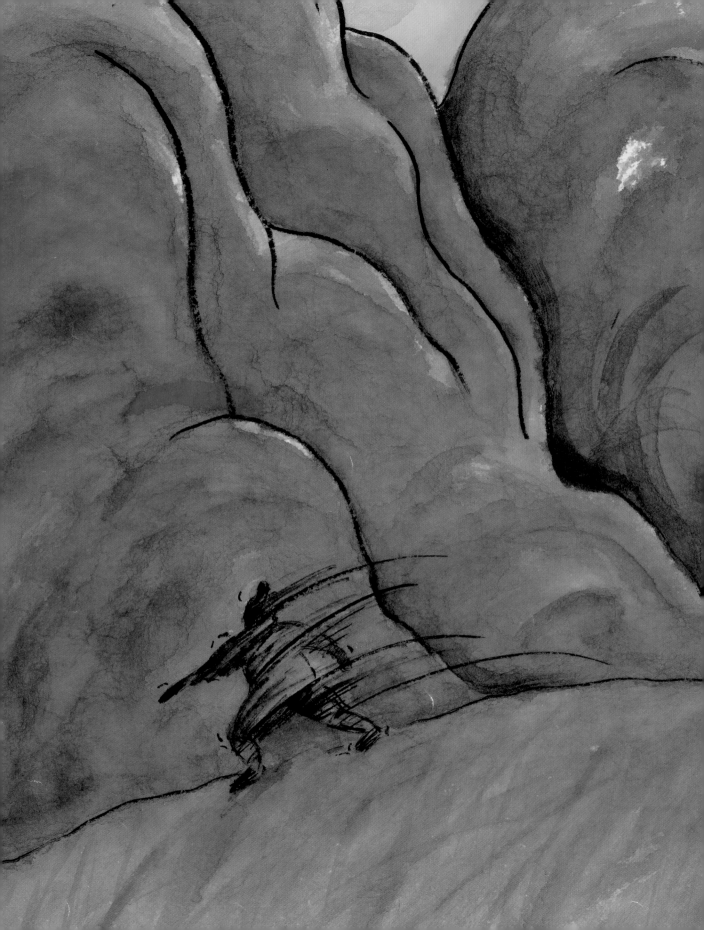

잠에서 깨어나 보니 When he woke, the orange sun hung low between the mountains. The old man clenched and un-clenched his fists. He bounced up on his toes, flexing the muscles in his legs. Never had he felt so calm, and yet full of energy.

Bounding off like a young gazelle, he ran all the way back to the forest and finished his entire day's work!

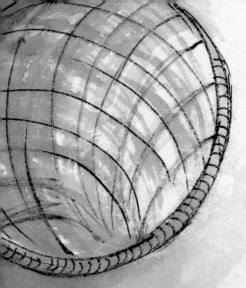

깜짝 놀라서

But when he walked through the door to his house that evening, the old man's wife stared at him openmouthed.

"Oh, my goodness, what has happened to you?" she cried.

"What? What is wrong?" asked the old man.

놀랍고 기쁨에 넘쳐

The old woman gently took her husband's fingers and pressed them against the smooth, firm skin of his face. Then the old man's jaw dropped, and he realized what had happened. He had become young again! Shaking with excitement, he told his wife all about the bluebird's song and the magic spring. They both cried tears of joy.

다음날 아침

In the morning the man led his wife back to the valley and showed her the spring. After one quick drink, she too became strong and limber again. Then the handsome young couple returned home together, full of plans for the future.

욕심쟁이는 궁금하여

Now the greedy neighbor watched all the changes in the couple. One day he approached them as they worked in their garden.

"Good fortune seems to shine upon you, my friends," the neighbor said with a forced smile.

"Yes, it does," said the husband. "If only we had a child to share it with…"

"Yes, yes, yes," the old man said, cutting him off. "But how did you get to be so young and strong?"

The young man told him the secret of the spring and happily pointed the way. "All you need is one sip," the husband said.

욕심쟁이는 단숨에 달려가

But the greedy old neighbor was already off, eager to get to the spring. Sure enough, he soon came to the valley and found the spring bubbling between the rocks. He fell to his knees, scooping water up to his face with both hands, gulping and slurping until he'd drunk right down to the bottom of the spring.

Then, his full belly sloshing with every step, he found a spot in the shade and fell into a deep, deep sleep.

밤이 깊어지자 That evening, as the hour grew late and their neighbor had not returned to the village, the husband and wife grew concerned. Together they went out searching for him, and as they neared the valley, they heard a loud cry.

오래도록 행복하게

They quickened their step and
found, wrapped in the cloak of
the greedy old neighbor, a tiny
baby, kicking its legs helplessly.
The wife picked the baby up and
held him against her shoulder.
Right then his crying stopped.

So the husband and wife took
the baby home. They raised him
with love.

And they all lived happily
ever after.

G. P. Putnam's Sons, a division of The Putnam & Grosset Group,
200 Madison Avenue, New York, NY 10016.
Published simultaneously in Canada.
Printed in Hong Kong by South China Printing Co. (1988) Ltd.
Book design by Gunta Alexander. The text is set in Novarese.
Library of Congress Cataloging-in-Publication Data
Rhee, Nami.   Magic spring: a Korean folktale/retold and illustrated by Nami Rhee.
p.   cm.   ''A Whitebird book.''   Summary: An old man and his wife discover a fountain of youth
and benefit from its magic, but the water has a different effect on their greedy neighbor.
[1. Folklore—Korea.]   I. Title. PZ8.1.R375Mag   1993   92-7728 CIP AC   398.21—dc20 [E]
ISBN 0-399-22420-3
10 9 8 7 6 5 4 3 2 1
First Impression